Bella Donna

Ruth Symes thinks the next best thing to being magic is writing stories about magic. She lives in Bedfordshire and when she isn't writing she can be found by the river walking her dogs, Traffy and Bella (who are often in the river).

Find out more at: www.ruthsymes.com

Marion Lindsay has always loved stories and pictures, so it made perfect sense when she decided to become a children's book illustrator, and she won the Egmont Best New Talent Award. She lives and works in Cambridge, and in her spare time paints glass and makes jewellery.

Find out more at: www.marionlindsay.co.uk

Bella Donna

Witch Camp

Ruth Symes

Illustrated by Marion Lindsay

Piccadilly Press

For the whole Winter Family,
plus Erin, Nara, Hannah, Georgie and Caitlin,
as well as Amy and her cat called Wish.
R.S.

For Carina,
with love and thanks.
M.L.

First published in Great Britain in 2013
by Piccadilly Press Ltd,
A Templar/Bonnier publishing company
Deepdene Lodge, Deepdene Avenue,
Dorking, Surrey, RH5 4AT
www.piccadillypress.co.uk

Text copyright © Ruth Symes, 2013
Illustrations copyright © Marion Lindsay, 2013

A catalogue record for this book is available
from the British Library

ISBN: 978 1 84812 310 6

1 3 5 7 9 10 8 6 4 2

Printed and bound by CPI Group (UK) Ltd, Croydon, CR0 4YY
Cover design by Simon Davis
Cover illustration by Marion Lindsay

Chapter 1

Where do witchlings go for their summer holidays? They go to Witch Camp. Or at least that's where my cousin Verity's going – and it's just about the only thing she can talk about!

'Did you know Witch Camp has been

running for almost a hundred years?' she said, as soon as she walked through the front door for our Saturday morning spell-casting class.

My tabby cat, Pegatha, greeted Verity with a hiss. She doesn't like her much.

'Yes, you already told me — twice,' I said, but Verity wasn't listening.

'And it always begins on the Eve of Lammas — the thirty-first of July,' she continued.

Lammas is a celebration of the first fruits of the harvest and it's followed a few weeks later by the Barley Moon celebration when there is a full moon. Witches have eight big festivals each year and at Coven Road we celebrate all of them. Plus we have lots of other parties to celebrate all sorts of different things too. Witches love parties!

Verity flipped through the pages of the Witch Camp brochure she'd brought with her.

Thirteen boy and girl witchlings of spell-casting

age are invited each year,' she read. 'So many want to go, but they don't have room for everyone.'

'I don't want to go,' I reminded her. I had no intention of going to Witch Camp.

But Verity just waved the brochure in my face. 'You can't even begin to imagine how fantastic it's going to be, Bella,' she said, her eyes shining. 'Witch Camp is like going to a Coven

Road party every single day, only better! It's the most magical place ever.'

Sometimes Verity says things just to make me jealous, so I thought she was probably exaggerating about Witch Camp. It was very hard for me to imagine anywhere could be more magical than Coven Road.

Before I lived here I used to live at Templeton Children's Home, which isn't magical at all. But then one wonderful day Lilith came along and she adopted me. I didn't know she was a witch at first or that Coven Road was a road where only witches lived. If I had known, I probably would have burst with happiness! I'd wanted to be a witch for as long as I could remember, even though I didn't know I actually *was* a witch – or 'witchling' to be precise, which is a young witch – until Lilith told me.

'Hello, Verity,' said Lilith, coming out of the

kitchen where she'd been getting the cauldron ready for our lesson.

'Look at all the great things I'm going to get to do at Witch Camp, Auntie Lilith,' Verity said, pointing at a page showing witchlings running through an emerald field full of amazing flowers and butterflies. 'I can't wait to go.'

I watched as Lilith took the brochure from Verity and slowly turned the pages.

'When I was a witchling I used to love toasting marshmallows around the rainbow campfire,' she said, and then she smiled. 'One year, a boy witchlings said he ate a hundred marshmallows in one night. I don't know if he really did or not

but he certainly had a bad stomach-ache the next day!'

I'd never seen a rainbow fire or toasted a marshmallow in one. It did sound like fun. But not fun enough to make me want to go to Witch Camp.

'Do they have a picture of the rainbow fire?' I asked, leaning forward so I could see the pictures too.

'No, but there's one of the fireworks,' Verity said. 'Most of all I'm looking forward to learning how to cast lots of new spells, Auntie Lilith.'

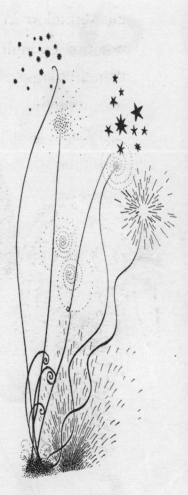

'Oh,' I said, in a small voice. I'd have liked to do that too. Spell-casting lessons are so much fun that Verity and I both wish we could have more of them. We're allowed to have one a week, on Saturday mornings, and we're only allowed to learn one new spell, at the most, during it.

Getting spells wrong can have terrible effects, so it's the best way to make sure each one is learnt properly.

According to the brochure, at Witch Camp the only-one-spell-a-week rule was temporarily suspended.

'Would you like to learn one of the spells I was taught when I went to Witch Camp?' Lilith asked us.

'Yes!' Verity and I both said together.

'Fish,' said Pegatha.

To most people Pegatha looks like just an ordinary tabby cat,  but she isn't ordinary at all. Recently we found out that she is a true witch's cat, and these are very rare. True witches' cats get to choose their own witch to live with, and Pegatha chose me! They have their own sort of magic, but no one really knows much about it. It's very mysterious.

So I have my very own special witch's cat even though I'm still a witchling. I only guessed the truth when she started trying to talk, and she can only say one word: fish. I think she likes saying fish because it's her favourite food!

Our other cats – Mystica, Amelka, Bazeeta and Brimalkin – sat on the bookshelves watching us, but pretending they weren't really. They're just regular Siamese cats, though they still act all superior.

'I can't quite remember the spell,' Lilith said. 'I'll just go and fetch my grimoire.' That is a special book where witches write down all their spells. Lilith's grimoire is so full it's almost

bursting.

'I can't wait to go back to Witch Camp,' Verity said. 'No one wanted to leave Witch Camp last year. Everyone was soooo sad on our last day.'

I shook my head because I was sure I'd be

more than happy to leave Witch Camp. I didn't want to go there in the first place, not one tiny little bit, not even if they taught us a hundred new spells. I didn't want to leave Lilith, or Pegatha, or the other cats, or Coven Road for two days, let alone two weeks.

Verity didn't like me shaking my head. She's a few years older than I am and she always thinks she's right about everything.

Sometimes Verity can be really nice but sometimes she can be just plain nasty.

'If you were at Witch Camp, you wouldn't want to leave either, Bella Donna,' she insisted, putting her hands on her hips and emphasising every word. 'You're just pretending you don't want to go because you haven't been invited! They must have forgotten about you because you're so new to the witch world. But any witchling who was lucky enough to be invited and did get to go to Witch Camp would never ever want to leave . . .'

Chapter 2

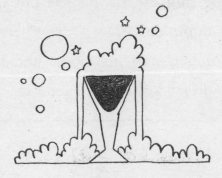

What Verity didn't know was that I *had* been invited to Witch Camp. I'd just decided to pretend I hadn't. The invitation had come while Lilith had been tending the herbs in the back garden, so she hadn't seen it arrive. I'd guessed what it was though, as soon as I saw the envelope drop through the letterbox.

We have our very own Coven Road witch postman. A non-witch one would never have been able to find our street! Our witch postman delivers the mail on his bicycle but he prefers riding his flying carpet.

The Witch Camp invitation had butterflies on it that danced about as I read it.

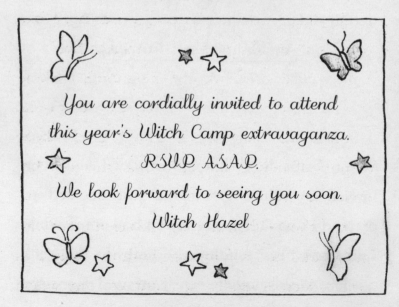

You are cordially invited to attend this year's Witch Camp extravaganza.
RSVP ASAP.
We look forward to seeing you soon.
Witch Hazel

Only I didn't want to RSVP ASAP. I didn't want to reply at all. Witch Camp was the last place in the world I wanted to go. I was really looking forward to spending the first summer holidays since being adopted by Lilith at home in Coven Road. It was going to be very nice learning some new spells with Lilith without Verity being at the class too. Without her there I could learn the spells that I most wanted to. I really didn't want to have to go away. I was already in the only place I wanted to be.

I'd stared down at the invitation, wishing that it had never even dropped through the letterbox. If only Witch Hazel could have forgotten about me and left me off her invitation list.

And that's when a good idea had crept into my head. I had run upstairs with the invitation and hidden it under my mattress and when

Lilith came back inside I didn't say anything about it. So long as no one knew I'd been invited to Witch Camp then I wouldn't have to go to Witch Camp.

Pegatha saw the whole thing, of course, but I could trust her to keep a secret.

'Actually, I'm glad I'm not going to Witch Camp. I wouldn't want to go even if I was invited,' I told Verity, as Lilith came downstairs with her grimoire.

'You would,' Verity shouted.

'I wouldn't!' I shouted back.

Pegatha growled deep in her throat at Verity.

'Girls!' Lilith said, sighing. She doesn't like it

when Verity and I quarrel – which happens a lot because Verity is soooooo annoying. 'The spell I want to teach you today is called a glamour spell,' Lilith said. 'Can you stop arguing for long enough to learn it?'

'Yes,' Verity and I said.

'Fish,' said Pegatha.

Verity and I glared daggers at each other as we followed Lilith to the cauldron.

'What's a glamour spell?' I asked Lilith.

'A glamour spell makes something appear to look better than it really is,' Lilith said.

'Like an illusion?' asked Verity.

'Sometimes, yes.'

'Then I don't need a spell. I'm already much more glamorous than Bella,' Verity said.

'No you're not!' I said, although secretly I knew she was. Verity's very pretty with jet black hair and lots of nice clothes.

'In the story
of Cinderella, a
glamour spell is put
on the kitchen girl so
she looks like a princess,'
Lilith told us.
'Do all fairy stories have
spells in them?' I asked her.
Lilith frowned. 'Maybe not *all* but I
think lots of them do,' she said.

'Is there a spell to make yourself look
exactly like another person?' Verity asked
Lilith. 'Then Bella Donna could look like me!'
she said, smiling.

I really wanted to tell her that I would never
want to look like her, but I managed to stop
myself.

'Yes,' Lilith said, and then she frowned. 'It's an
imitation spell. Although I've never used it. It's a

very powerful spell that only the most experienced witches can do – witches who are a lot more advanced than me.'

That's one of the things I really like about Lilith. Unlike many grown-ups, she doesn't pretend she can do more than she really can, or that she knows more than she really does.

'It's far too advanced for you to learn yet,' Lilith said, 'and it can be very dangerous. It's the sort of spell that's best left to someone like Zorelda.'

Zorelda's the Grand Sorceress of Coven Road and you can tell she's super powerful just by looking at her. Not that she's big or has flames coming out of her fingertips or anything (although I expect she could if she wanted to) but there's an aura about her that's so strong it gives me goosebumps sometimes.

The truth is she's more than a little bit scary. No wise witchling would ever even think about trying to cast a Zorelda-type of spell.

'Yes – what if you got stuck?' I said to Verity. 'You could end up being someone else forever.' It didn't sound like a good idea to me at all.

Pegatha rubbed her little cat face against my hand to show she agreed with me.

'Exactly,' Lilith said. 'Now would you like to give the glamour spell a try?'

'Yes!' we both said.

'We'll need tangle-root, white and black candles, lavender, poppy leaves . . .'

Lilith read out the ingredients and Verity and I found what we needed as fast as we could. Once we had everything it was time to cast the spell.

'Bags I go first,' Verity said, as we stood around the cauldron.

She dropped half the ingredients we'd gathered into the cauldron. Then Lilith started to say the spell words and Verity chanted them after her, as she focused in her mind on the changes the

glamour spell should make. It's impossible to write the words down, but this is as close as I can come: '*Fristoria frandillio fristomnia fristal.*'

As I watched, Verity started to change, just a little. The effect was subtle and I might not have noticed the differences if I hadn't been looking for them. Her hair got super shiny and thicker and her eyes got bigger and seemed to sparkle.

'Is it working?' Verity said.

I nodded.

'Yes,' Lilith said with a smile. 'You look especially beautiful.'

But a few seconds later the glamour spell had faded and Verity went back to her usual self again.

'You do it now, Bella,' Verity said.

I dropped the rest of the ingredients into the cauldron, stirred and chanted the spell. '*Fristoria frandillio fristomnia fristal.*'

I didn't feel any different but I knew it must be working because I heard Verity gasp and Pegatha jumped up onto the bookcases to be with the other cats.

I felt taller and more sophisticated and confident. When I looked down I saw I was wearing sparkly golden shoes. My hair was curled and I had a tiara balanced on my head, and a ring with a big jewel in it. I laughed and Verity scowled and folded her arms and made a 'Huh!' sound.

Although I'm much less experienced at spell-casting than Verity, my spells usually turn out much stronger than hers do (Lilith says it's to do with how much magic I have in me) so I remained my glamorous new self for a good five minutes.

Verity didn't like the new me much.

'It's not fair!' she said. 'I wish I'd looked in the mirror so I could have seen what I looked like before my spell faded.'

Lilith shook her head. 'A mirror can't be fooled by a spell,' she said.

Pegatha walked back over to me and
rubbed her furry head against my face.
She liked me just as much with
the spell or without.

'I bet Pegatha would love Witch Camp,'
Verity said. 'She might even learn
another word.'

'What?' I asked her. What was Verity
talking about? 'Can witches' cats go
to Witch Camp?'

'It says so in the brochure,' said Verity.

'It does?'

'Yup, on page two.'

'Yes, of course witches' cats are allowed
at Witch Camp too,' Lilith said. 'Only
witches' cats, though, not regular cats.
You can't separate a witch's cat from its
witch for long – it wouldn't be fair.'

'No,' I said. I looked over at Pegatha

cleaning her whiskers. She'd probably
really enjoy Witch Camp and it wasn't
fair for her to have to miss it because of
me. I raced up the stairs.

'Bella, are you OK?' Lilith called after me.

But I didn't answer her. I went into
my room, pushed up the mattress,
pulled out the invitation in its
envelope and ran back down again.

'I've been invited to Witch Camp,' I said,
and I handed the invitation to Lilith.

'At last,' she said. 'I was wondering
when you would show me this.'

'You knew I had it?' I said.

'Of course. Witch Hazel wrote to ask
for my permission to allow you to go.'

Verity had her hands on her hips.
'Why didn't you tell me?' she said.

I didn't want to answer her. I couldn't

believe what Lilith had told me. 'You knew all the time?' I asked Lilith.

Lilith nodded and put her arm around my shoulders.

'Why didn't you say so?'

'Because I was sure there must be a very good reason for you not telling me and that you would once you were ready,' Lilith replied.

'I wanted to spend the summer here with you and Pegatha,' I said. 'I'd miss you both so much . . .'

'You should have told me,' Verity said, ignoring what we were saying. She sounded a bit cross.

Lilith hugged me to her. 'I'll miss you too but I think you should go. I'm sure you'll enjoy Witch Camp very much, and you won't even have to miss Pegatha, because she'll be there too. Although she'll probably be the only one.

Most witchlings aren't lucky enough to have their very own witch's cat, you know.'

'Now I'll have to babysit both you and Pegatha at Witch Camp,' Verity said, and she gave a loud sigh.

'We don't need you to look after us,' I laughed. 'Pegatha and I can take care of ourselves.'

Pegatha wound herself in and out of my legs and purred.

'We're going to Witch Camp!' I told her, as I stroked her soft fur.

'Fish,' said Pegatha.

Chapter 3

When I first came to live here, before I knew I was really a witchling, I didn't realise there was anything unusual about Lilith or Coven Road. To me our house just looked like every other house around, and the neighbours seemed nice

but not really unusual
in any way.
How wrong
could I be!
I'd been living with
Lilith for a few weeks
before I found out
that actually the
houses in Coven Road
looked very magical
and unusual, and that every
single one of our neighbours
was a witch. Once a month, at
midnight, all the witches cast a
spell together that makes
Coven Road look like any
other perfectly normal street
to non-witch visitors, and even
hides the entrance to Coven

Road to anyone just
passing by who isn't a witch.

Lilith and me and our little
cat family live in a beautiful
thatched cottage with roses
round the door that are
constantly changing colour.
The other witches here live in
tree houses and ice palaces and
pirate ships – and whenever they
want to, they can change
their house into something
that looks quite different. I
wouldn't want to change
our house though. I think
it's perfect just the way it is.

Being a witchling is so
exciting that it's a shame I
can't tell my school friends

anything about it, although they probably wouldn't believe me if I did. It's one of the rules of living in Coven Road that you can't tell anyone about it, or about being a witch.

The following Friday was the last day of term, and as I walked into my classroom, everyone was talking about what they were going to be doing during the summer holidays.

I sit next to Angela, who I've known ever since we were at nursery school although we've only really become friends recently. Before that she just thought I was weird for wanting to be a witch and wearing black all the time, and I thought she was weird for always wearing pink. I still want to be a witch and she still wears pink but now we just accept each other's differences and are good friends.

Angela was going to a dance school for part of the summer.

'Mum's bought me some new tap-dancing shoes,' Angela said. 'Guess what colour they are?'

It wasn't hard. 'Er . . . pink?' I asked.

'Correct!' she said, smiling.

I really wanted to tell her about Witch Camp but I couldn't because everything about Coven Road and me being a witchling has to remain a secret – and that includes where I'm going on holiday!

My other friend, Sam, dashed into class just as the bell for the start of lessons rang. Sam and I have been friends ever since we were babies together at Templeton Children's Home. Shortly after I was adopted by Lilith, Sam was adopted by Trevor and Tracey. They live at the Woodland Wildlife Centre and are just as mad about animals as he is.

Sam is the only one at school who knows that I'm a witchling and the truth about Coven Road. It was an accident that he found out, and he had to make a promise to Zorelda that he would never, ever tell. I know he won't break his promise. He wouldn't dare. Zorelda could  turn him into a frog or a mouse or anything she liked in the blink of an eye.

'I'm late because Bobby went running off after squirrels on our walk again,' Sam said as he sat down behind me. 'I told him they wouldn't want to play with him but he didn't listen.'

Bobby's the latest addition to Sam's family. He's the most cute, sweet, little yellow Labrador puppy.

Our teacher, Mrs Pearce, walked into class then and we all had to stop talking and face the front.

'Good morning, class,' Mrs Pearce said. 'I hope you're all looking forward to your summer holidays.'
'We are, miss.'
'And that you won't miss school too badly.'
'We won't, miss.'
Sam put his hand up. 'Where are you going for your holiday, Mrs Pearce?' he asked her.
'I'm going on a walking holiday in

the Lake District,' Mrs Pearce said.

'Oooh, watch out for adders,' Sam said. 'You might be lucky enough to see one if you look carefully.'

'I will,' Mrs Pearce said, looking slightly worried.

Sam was too busy thinking about adders to notice. 'They're very shy,' he said, thoughtfully. 'And not at all aggressive. You probably won't spot one because it'll most likely wriggle away as soon as you get near it.'

'Good,' Mrs Pearce said.

'And even if an adder did bite you, you might not notice because an adder bite can feel just like a bramble scratch,' Sam said.

'Right, well, let's get on now,' Mrs Pearce said. 'Who —'

'You'd know though after about an hour when the bite becomes red and swollen,' Sam added.

Mrs Pearce looked very worried now.

'Once you start to feel sick it'd be best to call an ambulance,' Sam said. 'Just in case . . .'

Mrs Pearce had turned pale and I didn't blame her at all. I hoped there wouldn't be any snakes at Witch Camp. Perhaps there was a spell for keeping them away.

'But you probably won't see one,' Sam continued. 'Snakes, and most other wild animals and reptiles, are much more frightened of us than we are of them.' He smiled sweetly at Mrs Pearce but Mrs Pearce didn't smile back.

'I'm going to India, miss,' Ellen said. 'They have cobras and vipers and they're both venomous. If one of those bit you it would be much worse than an adder bite. I'm really frightened of them.'

'The best thing to do when confronted by a frightened or wild animal is to act like

you're not scared of it,' Sam said. That
sounded a lot easier said than done to me!

'I think that's quite enough about snakes for
today,' Mrs Pearce said.

'I'm much more worried about meeting a
tiger than a snake, anyway,' Ellen added.

'We're going to Disneyworld in Florida and
they have alligators – or is it crocodiles? It
might be both!' said Rajni.

'Alligators in Florida, of course,' said Sam. 'If

I had to choose, I'd rather meet an alligator than a crocodile,' Sam said. 'Alligators are usually more scared of people and will run away but some crocodiles, especially big salt water crocodiles, can be man-eaters!'

Soon everyone was trying to outdo each other with how dangerous and scary their summer holidays were going to be.

'My gran has the biggest spiders in her bath. When I went to stay with her last year one of them was bigger than my whole hand,' Tony told us.

I gave a shudder because I'm not very keen on spiders, especially when they scuttle about.

'My mum says there's a ghost where she works,' Jane said.

'There's a story about a pair of dancing shoes that appear at the dance school,' said Angela. 'When you put them on they make you dance and dance and your feet won't stop dancing, however tired you get, until you die.'

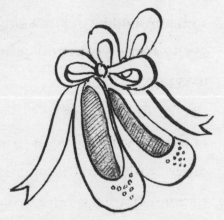

Sam chirped in with, 'There's bound to be blood-sucking leeches in the pond we're clearing on our conservation holiday. They clamp onto their victims and leave a three-cornered bite.'

Mrs Pearce clapped her hands as the noise in the classroom got louder and louder.

'Quieten down now,' she said. 'I think it's safe to assume that all of us are going to have very interesting holidays this year.'

I just smiled. I knew my holiday would be even more exciting than anyone could imagine!

Chapter 4

The days before I had to leave for Witch Camp flew past as I played with Pegatha and tried, unsuccessfully, to teach her to say my name. I also practised riding on my broomstick and nearly managed to do a handstand on it once

– although I was a bit wobbly.

Lilith showed me how to make delicious chocolate and peanut butter slices and I ate so many I felt a bit sick.

As well as spending time at home I visited Sam at the Woodland Wildlife Centre and played with Bobby.

I admired Angela's new clothes for dance camp and went shopping with Lilith. We bought lots of lovely new black outfits for Witch Camp, plus a feathery pink mouse for Pegatha to take with us and four yellow and blue mice

for Mystica, Amelka, Brimalkin and Bazeeta. You might think we could just magic all these things up, but that's not the way it works. Most of the time we go shopping like everyone else and I'm glad we do. I like shopping with Lilith and choosing new clothes and presents for our cats.

'You'll be having so much fun you'll barely have time to miss us,' Lilith said.

But I shook my head because I knew that wouldn't be true. Just thinking about going away still gave me a bit of a lump in my throat.

The doorbell rang and Lilith went to see who it could be. When she came back she was holding a black and silver envelope addressed to her. The silver on it was so shiny it looked like it must be real silver.

Lilith looked a bit flustered.

'What is it?' I asked her.

'Well, it looks like . . . Only it can't be . . .'

This wasn't like Lilith at all.

'What is it?' I asked again.

'I think it's a letter from the Witches' Council.'

I was bursting with curiosity. 'Open it,' I said.

Lilith carefully tore the envelope open, took out the letter inside it and read aloud.

Dear Ms Sorciere,
There is a vacancy at the
Barley Moon Sorcery Convention
in August.
Your name was put forward
and you have been selected as a member
of the Thirteen of Thirteen.
We very much hope you
will accept the role.
With kindest regards,
The Witches' Council

Lilith sank down into an armchair. 'Oh my goodness,' she said. 'It really is a big honour and I'm not sure I deserve it.'

'Of course you do, you're the best witch in the world!' I told her.

'Thank you, Bella Donna, but I'm not sure everyone else would agree with you.'

'So now we'll both be going away!' I said.

Lilith looked like she still couldn't quite believe she'd been invited to the Sorcery Convention. 'Mine's only for two nights, but it is still very exciting,' she said, and her face was beaming. 'I'll need to get something new to wear. Something black – or maybe it should be silver.'

'Will Zorelda be going?'

'Oh yes, she's at the top of the list,' Lilith said, turning over the invitation and looking at all the names of the other witches invited. 'I can hardly believe they've chosen me . . .'

Later I heard Lilith humming to herself as she went around the cottage, and I knew she was happy and that made me happy.

🕷️ 🕷️ 🕷️

The days before Witch Camp flew by and before I knew it, it was Lammas Eve.

I'd almost finished packing my suitcase and Pegatha had her feathery pink mouse beside her on the bed, ready to go, when Lilith came into my room and handed me a beautiful small crystal ball.

'Do you remember the finding spell?' she asked me.

'Yes.' I hardly ever forget spells once I've been taught them. I don't know why, because I forget lots of other things, but for some reason I'm always able to remember spells. It's the only thing I've ever really been good at. Perhaps it's

because I like spells so much.

'Well, you can use this to contact me while
I'm at the Barley Moon Sorcery Convention, if
you need to.'

Apparently there was so much magic there

that normal phones didn't work properly, and were likely to end up turning themselves into something else anyway.

I clasped the ball in my hand but then I had a worrying thought. 'What if I lose it?' I said.

'I'm sure you won't lose it,' Lilith said, giving my shoulder a reassuring squeeze. 'But if you did, then any glass, or even an ice cube, would work. You just need something clear. Crystal balls are commonly used but what matters most is how badly you want to get in contact with the person you're trying to reach. Even the very best crystal ball won't work as well as a piece of glass and a heart that's true.'

That's the thing about spells – the intent behind the spell is often what matters most.

'And, of course, whoever you're trying to contact needs to want to be contacted, otherwise it's pointless.'

I nodded. 'Like when we were trying to find you,' I said to Pegatha, 'and you didn't want to be found.'

When Pegatha first started realising she was magical, she got very confused and ran away. Now she licked my hand, looked me straight in the eye and I'm sure she smiled.

She is such a funny little cat.

Lilith had made my favourite munchkin risotto as a special going-away dinner.

'Was Witch Hazel in charge of Witch Camp when you were a witchling?' I asked her, as we ate.

'Yes, I think she's been there almost as long as Witch Camp's been running,' Lilith said. 'She's such a sweet witch, Bella, and makes everyone feel at home. I'm sure you're going to like her. And she loves cats, so I'm sure Pegatha will like her too.'

'Fish,' said Pegatha.

At ten to midnight, Verity knocked on our front door. She was holding her broomstick in her hand.

'Ready?' she said. At first Verity hadn't seemed totally pleased that I was going to be

coming to Witch Camp too but now I think
she was glad to have someone to travel with.

The only way to get there was by broomstick
and I picked up mine.

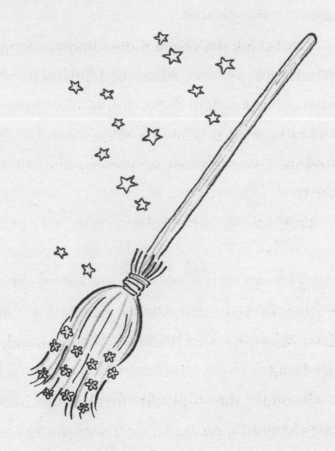

All witches' broomsticks come from the same forest. It's called Witchwood. No trees are ever chopped down there but if a branch chooses to become a witch's broomstick, it drops to the ground.

The other amazing thing about witches' broomsticks is that when they're happy they often blossom with flowers. Lilith's broomstick blossoms with lilies and Verity's blossoms with roses but mine has a thousand different wild flowers. When lots of witches are flying together, their broomsticks look so pretty. Sometimes it's important that the broomsticks don't bloom even when they are happy, though – like when the Broomstick Riders are doing their flying tricks. Otherwise there'd be petals all over the place, which would look pretty, but might make it hard for them to see where they were going.

Verity didn't have any luggage with her because she'd sent it on ahead. It would be cruel to expect our broomsticks to carry us and our heavy suitcases as well. I'd packed so much in mine I was sure my broomstick wouldn't have been able to fly with both me and Pegatha and my suitcase on it anyway. I'd even packed the witch mobile that hangs in my bedroom window. It's been

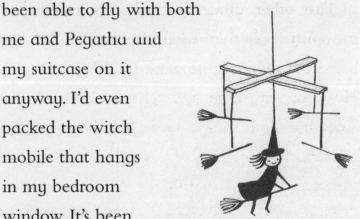

with me ever since I was a baby.

'Where's your Witch Camp luggage label?' Verity asked me.

I pulled the shimmering silvery label out of my pocket and she took it from me.

'You sure this is all you want to take?' she said.

I nodded. I'd have liked to take Lilith and Mystica, Bazeeta, Brimalkin and Amelka with me, and Sam and Angela too. But of course that wasn't possible.

Verity was about to stick the label on my suitcase when Lilith said, 'Wait!' She smiled at me as she pulled a beautiful photo frame from behind her back. 'One more thing to pack.'

Inside the frame was a photograph of Lilith standing in front of the bookshelves with Mystica, Amelka, Bazeeta and Brimalkin peeping out behind her.

'Thank you,' I said, as I threw my arms round Lilith and hugged her. I had such a big lump in my throat that I could hardly speak.

Verity shoved the photo frame into the front pocket of my suitcase and stuck the label on. No sooner had she done so than my suitcase disappeared in a puff of sparkling smoke.

'It'll be waiting for you in your cabin at Witch Camp,' she said.

But I knew that already because it said so in the brochure.

The clock on the wall struck midnight.

'Time for us to go,' Verity said. 'We don't want to be late.'

Pegatha's little claws clung onto the broomstick as we flew up into the dark night sky.

All witches' broomsticks have personalities of their own and mine is the bravest, most loyal broomstick I know. Once it even saved me by flying up the chimney when I'd cast a very dangerous spell by mistake. I was very glad that it was coming with us because I was feeling a bit scared and worried about going away. But at least I'd have Pegatha and my broomstick, plus Verity of course, only sometimes Verity can be a bit mean.

I looked back to wave goodbye to Lilith and saw her mopping away a tear. When she saw me waving, she waved her hanky at me instead.

Chapter 5

I didn't know the way to Witch Camp but my broomstick did. It followed a magical sky path of twinkling stars, and we soon saw more witchlings flying ahead of us. Other witchlings were flying behind us as well. Everyone was

very excited. They laughed and called out to each other.

'Hi, Ophelia, haven't seen you since last year!'

'Nice new broomstick, Eddie.'

'Hope we get to learn loads of new spells, Mia.'

I hoped so too. As I'm always saying, learning new spells is one of my very favourite

things to do. I felt all tingly with excitement as we flew on and on through the beautiful corridor of glittering stars.

When I saw the twins Jezelda and Morgana ahead of us, I wasn't sure whether I should say hello or not. Jezelda and Morgana look identical and the only way to tell them apart is by their hair – Morgana usually wears her long black hair in one plait and Jezelda wears hers in two. I'd met Jezelda and Morgana once before when we'd all been in a spell-casting contest together. Jezelda had won the contest with her dragon spell. First she'd made a dragon egg appear and then the egg hatched and the next moment Jezelda was flying around the room on her very own dragon. It really was the most amazing spell.

Morgana came second with her picnic spell, which made everyone's favourite sandwich magically appear. I'd made my hair turn into rainbow colours and grow and grow until it spread out across the floor. I'd been really disappointed when I'd only come third, even though I hadn't been learning magic for very long, and I knew Jezelda and Morgana's spells were much more impressive than mine.

I thought maybe I wouldn't say hello to Jezelda and Morgana. They came from a long line of witches and probably knew everyone already, and I still felt a bit jealous of them.

But then Morgana spotted me and started waving.

'Merry meet, Bella Donna,' she shouted.

'Merry meet' is a special witches' greeting. I think it's a bit like saying, 'Good to see you.'

'Blessed be,' I called back.

That's the special witches' reply. Everyone says it and I think it means, 'Good to see you' too, as well as, 'I hope things are going well for you'.

'Nice to see you again, Bella Donna,' Jezelda said, swooping past and back again on her broomstick. That's when she saw Pegatha.

'You've got a witch's cat!' she said. 'Hey, Morgana, Bella's got her own witch's cat!' she shouted.

Morgana flew over.

'Her name's Pegatha,' I said.

'You're so lucky, Bella,' Morgana said, enviously. 'Witches' cats are so rare we might never get to have one.'

Jezelda tried to stroke Pegatha from her broomstick but it was too awkward. Pegatha miaowed a hello instead.

'Can't wait to say hello to Pegatha properly when we're on the ground,' she said, as she swished off.

I began to think that maybe Jezelda and Morgana weren't so bad after all.

'We're here!' Verity shouted a few minutes later, and we flew through the camp's golden snake gates and joined the rest of the witchlings

on the ground. There were six boy witchlings at the camp and seven girl witchlings.

'Adam!' Verity called out to a boy of about

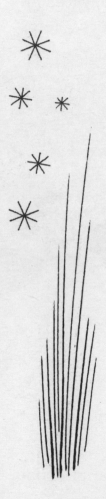

thirteen, with floppy brown
hair and green eyes.
'Hello, Verity,' he said, and I'm
sure if it hadn't been night-time
I'd have seen Verity blush.
'Wasn't sure if you'd be here this
year,' she said, trying to sound as
if she didn't care if he was there
or not.
A firework shot up into the sky,
as if welcoming us all.
'I'd never miss Witch Camp,'
Adam said, laughing.
'Once you've been . . .'
'. . . you'll never want to miss it,'
Verity finished, and the two of

them laughed and then Verity
kept on laughing.

'You're so funny, Adam,' she
said. Even though it wasn't all
that funny really.

Another firework raced into
the air and a cascade of firework
flowers came floating down.
Then another firework exploded,
and another and another. Soon
hundreds of fireworks burst into
colour in the night sky as we all
looked upwards and made
'Oooh' and 'Aaah' sounds. It was
so pretty.

Best of all, witches' fireworks

aren't like normal fireworks. They don't go off with loud bangs that frighten animals. The only sound witches' fireworks make is a soft tinkling of bells. Even Pegatha liked these fireworks.

'Fish,' she said, as she batted her paw at the sparkling lights raining around us.

The fireworks were followed by the Broomstick Riders display team. I could feel my broomstick quivering beside me as soon as it saw them and I knew it wanted to join in the display too.

As all broomsticks come from Witchwood and are said to be grown from the acorns of the first witch tree, I guess they are all related. Around me I could see other witchlings' broomsticks blooming with happiness and I smiled as hundreds of wild flowers suddenly appeared on mine.

I hugged Pegatha to me as we watched the

Broomstick Riders loop the loop and twirl and swirl and dance in the sky. Finally they flew their broomsticks into a pyramid shape as a cheer went up among the witchlings.

'They're amazing!' I said.

Next, a silver carriage led by two silver flying unicorns came floating into the sky and then drifted down to join us.

'It's Witch Hazel!' Verity cried.

Witch Hazel was small and round. She had rosy apple cheeks and she looked like she must laugh a lot because her face was all wrinkly.

Witch Hazel welcomed us all with the

special witches' greeting. 'Merry meet, dear witchlings, and welcome to Witch Camp. I am Witch Hazel and I hope you will all have an enlightening and happy time at this year's Witch Camp.'

'Fish,' Pegatha said, excitedly. 'Fish, fish, fish!'

'And who's this?' Witch Hazel asked me.

'Fish,' Pegatha said, and she pushed her head under Witch Hazel's hand for a stroke.

Witch Hazel smiled. 'What a lucky witchling you are, Bella Donna.'

I didn't know how she knew my name.

'I hope you stroke Pegatha a lot?'

And she knew Pegatha's name too.

'I do,' I told her.

'And let her sleep on your bed at night?'

'Always.'

'That cat's spoilt,' Verity said, and Pegatha hissed at her.

Verity wasn't pleased. 'She always does that!' she said, putting her hands on her hips.

Witch Hazel's eyes sparkled and I was sure she was trying hard not to laugh.

'Now, now, Verity, my dear,' she said, 'I'm sure you and Pegatha will be friends one day.'

Verity and Pegatha gave each other black looks.

Not only did Witch Hazel know my name and Pegatha and Verity's names, she seemed to know the names of everyone – even the other witchlings who hadn't been to Camp before.

It was after one o'clock in the morning, but

we weren't going to bed yet. Next there was a tour of the camp lit by bright silver, gold, pink and turquoise stars, left by the fireworks, to guide our way.

Pegatha ran after Witch Hazel as she stepped back into her carriage. When she reached her, Pegatha miaowed and Witch Hazel picked her up and then turned to me.

'Come and join us, Bella Donna,' she said.

I hurried over with my broomstick and climbed inside the silver carriage too.

'Th-thank you,' I managed to say, amazed to be given a ride.

The unicorns flew up into the sky and all the other witchlings followed behind us on their broomsticks. My broomstick flew behind us too – there wasn't room for it inside the carriage.

As we flew over the camp, Witch Hazel pointed out the cabins where we were to sleep.

She called them cabins but they were actually beautifully designed tree houses. Each of them was nestled in an ancient oak tree. The branches of the trees looked like they were hugging the tree houses.

I wondered which one I'd be in, and who I'd be sharing it with.

'That's where we have our meals,' Witch Hazel said, pointing out the dining cabin, which was shaped like a giant birthday cake with candles on the top.

We flew past the rainbow campfire, with its multi-coloured flames and sparkling stars that shot from it, and on past a fairy circle of blossoming trees, over a turquoise lake with dancing pink dolphins in it, and to the very edge of the camp.

Here Witch Hazel's carriage floated downwards and all the witchlings' broomsticks glided down and landed softly on the ground too.

I looked over at Verity as she pushed past another witchling so she could stand next to Adam.

Witch Hazel stepped out of her silver carriage. 'Welcome to the Ice Cave, everyone.'

We all crowded round to see it more clearly. A thick door of ice covered the entrance.

'The Ice Cave only opens its doors once every thirteen years,' she told us. 'And this is that year. A very special year – the thirteenth of thirteen.'

Pegatha wriggled out of my arms and jumped down as Witch Hazel faced the Ice Cave door, raised her arms up above her head and chanted, *'Corasalis chanali cartosos.'*

I gasped as, with a cracking and a creaking, the Ice Cave door slowly opened.

'This way,' Witch Hazel said, and we followed her inside.

I'd expected the Ice Cave to be dark but it wasn't. Thousands of glow-worms lit our way.

Still it was very cold and I was worried about Pegatha's little paws on the frozen ground. I could see her just ahead of me.

'Pegatha, come back,' I hissed. But she didn't stop. 'Excuse me,' I said to Verity as I brushed past her to reach Pegatha.

'Just because Witch Hazel let you ride in her carriage, it doesn't mean you're better than the rest of us,' she said.

'I didn't say I was.'

Verity always gets jealous if I get more attention than her. Sometimes I feel sorry for her but usually I just think she's being really childish.

I was about to pick Pegatha up so her paws wouldn't get frozen when she finally reached Witch Hazel and said 'Fish' pitifully.

'Oh, you poor little thing,' Witch Hazel said, and she scooped Pegatha up in her arms and wrapped her in her own warm cloak, from where Pegatha happily peeped out.

Pegatha was my cat and I should have felt a bit jealous that she wanted Witch Hazel to carry her instead of me, but for some reason I didn't mind at all. I was just glad Pegatha liked Witch Hazel so much. I liked her very much too.

Witch Hazel led us down a narrow tunnel until we came out into an amazing cavern. Icicles hung from the walls and stretching out

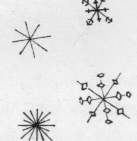

before us was a
lake of ice.
'How pretty!' I said.
As soon as I spoke,
snowflakes came out of my
mouth and danced in the air around me.

'Oh,' I said in surprise, and even more snowflakes appeared. I laughed and more snowflakes danced about as if they were silently laughing too.

I stopped laughing and put my hand over my mouth instead.

'It's quite all right,' Witch Hazel said, and she smiled her crinkly smile at me. As she spoke, her words turned into white snowflakes and flew off into the air too. 'Let's get to know each other. Call out your names and the covens you come from.'

Verity's friend spoke first.

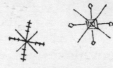

'Adam from Witches' Haven.'

'Ophelia. I'm from Witches'
Haven too.'

'Jezelda and Morgana from Merry
Meet Moor.'

'Eddic from Eastland End.'

'Toby and Brett from Warlock Weir.'

'Mia, Razi and Kye from Witch in the
Moon.'

'Verity from Coven Road.'

'Bella Donna from Coven Road too – and
that's my true witch's cat, Pegatha,' I said,
pointing at Pegatha.

'Fish,' said a small cat voice.

A girl of about my age with long
red hair was last. 'Opal from the
Cornish Cauldron,' she said, shyly.

Then she giggled at the

snowflakes her words had turned into.

Her snowflakes looked extra pretty when they danced. The rest of us laughed too and more and more snowflakes appeared and danced in the air around us until it felt like we were all giggling inside a snow globe.

I was so glad I'd been invited to Witch Camp.

Chapter 6

Finally it was time to go to bed.

'Here you are, little ones. Sleep tight, don't let the bed bugs bite,' Witch Hazel said, smiling, as she let Pegatha and me out of her carriage.

I was so tired I could hardly keep my eyes open.

'Fish,' Pegatha said, sleepily.

Our names were written on a sheet of parchment that was tied to the tree trunk. We were sharing a cabin with Verity, Jezelda, Morgana and Opal.

I looked round for Verity but I couldn't see her or Jezelda or Morgana so I put my broomstick in the broomstick rack and climbed up the wooden ladder.

From the ground the tree house looked quite small but inside it was much larger. There were five beds covered with multi-coloured patchwork quilts. Each had a dresser beside it and there was also a wardrobe for any of our clothes that needed to be hung up, and a little sink in one corner.

I saw my suitcase beside one of the beds. I hurried over and took the crystal ball from inside it. It was two o'clock in the morning but

Lilith had asked me to contact her as soon as I got a chance and this was my first chance.

'*Hoooonyaza …hekingabaal …hallazareti,*' I chanted.

Almost immediately Lilith's face appeared in the crystal. She was rubbing her eyes.

'How is it?' she asked me. 'Did you have a good journey? Are you all settled in?'

I was bubbling over with news. 'It's amazing!' I said, and I told her about the glittering star pathway and the fireworks and the Broomstick Riders and the Ice Cave and Witch Hazel. 'She welcomed us from the sky in a carriage with flying unicorns and then we got to go in her carriage and Pegatha totally loves her!' I finished.

I looked over at Pegatha who was already fast asleep on my pillow.

'I'm so glad you're having fun. Call me tomorrow if you can. Good night,' Lilith said, and her face inside the crystal ball faded away.

I was just hanging my witch mobile by my bed when Opal came into the cabin. She looked around her as if she couldn't quite believe she was really here either. I smiled at her.

'This place . . .' she said, and just smiled. 'I never imagined . . .'

I grinned. 'Me neither.'

'It's my first time here.'

'Mine too!' I replied.

'You're so lucky to have your own true witch's

cat,' she said, looking over at Pegatha, who was making cute little snoring sounds as she slept.

'I know,' I said, putting the crystal ball away.

Opal went over to her suitcase and started unpacking. 'I'm really glad to meet you, Bella,' she said. 'It felt before like everyone else knew each other already.'

I knew what she meant. Everywhere I'd looked, witchlings had been hugging and calling to each other. It did feel a bit like being the new girl at school, but at least now there were two of us.

'We'll soon know everyone too,' I told her.

As I unpacked my suitcase, I found that not only had Lilith given me the photo of her and the cats, she'd also put in some homemade cookies and my amber pendant.

I put the photograph on the little dresser beside my bed. I wanted their faces to be the last thing I saw at night and the first thing I saw in the morning.

Then I clasped the orangey pendant with black flecks in it round my neck.

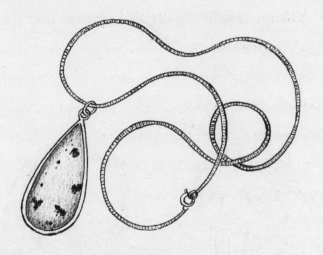

'What's that?' Opal asked.

'My mum gave it to me,' I said. 'Her mum gave it to her when she first started spell-casting.'

Opal didn't need to know I was adopted –

she would just think Lilith had always been my
mum, and for some reason I liked that.

'It's very pretty,' she said.

'It's made from amber,' I told her. I wanted to
wear it because it reminded me of home.

'Mmm and it smells like you've got cookies
too,' Opal said.

We were both really hungry so we shared Lilith's cookies. They were delicious! We'd eaten them all by the time Morgana and Jezelda came up the tree house ladder.

'Soooo tired,' said Morgana, yawning.

'Must sleep,' said Jezelda, flopping onto her bed.

Ten minutes later, Verity came up the ladder.

'Where've you been?' I asked her. The rest of us had cleaned our teeth and were just about to climb into bed.

Jezelda and Morgana exchanged a look.

'It's quite a walk back from the boy witchlings' side, isn't it?' Morgana said.

'It's easier if you fly on your broomstick,' Verity replied, and then put her hand over her mouth when she realised she'd just confirmed their suspicions. Then she shrugged. 'We had a lot to talk about.'

'Is Adam your boyfriend?' I asked her.

'No.'

'But she'd like him to be,' Jezelda said.

And then we all laughed – even Verity.

Chapter 7

When I woke up the next day the sun was streaming into our tree house and Pegatha was snuggled up beside me as usual.

Sleepily I stretched out my fingers to touch the photograph of Lilith, Mystica, Brimalkin,

Bazeeta and Amelka.

'Morning, Bella,' Opal said.

'They let us sleep in late, but it's almost lunchtime,' said Jezelda as she joined Morgana at the tree house door. 'Verity's already gone.'

'I'll wait for you,' said Opal, as I threw back the bed cover and jumped out of bed and got ready faster than I ever had before.

The meal cabin was full of hungry witchlings when Opal, Pegatha and I arrived. Wherever I looked there was just about every food you could imagine and lots I'd never tasted before, like walnut pancakes, noodle surprise and rosehip sauce. Pride of place was given to a huge fountain of all sorts of different berries in the middle of the room.

There were so many different foods it was hard to choose what to eat but Pegatha knew exactly what she wanted.

'Fish!' she told the magic buffet table, and immediately a small plate of fish appeared in front of her.

'How did that happen?' Opal asked. 'I've never seen a table do that before!'

I was about to tell her about the one we have in Coven Road when Verity came over.

'Where've you been?' she said to me. 'I was looking for you.'

She had Adam with her.

'Hello, Bella Donna,' he said.

He looked down at Pegatha eating her breakfast. 'I've never met a witch's cat before,' he said. He went to stroke Pegatha but Verity pulled his hand away.

'Not while she's eating,' she said. 'Pegatha's grumpy at the best of times.'

'No she isn't,' I said.

Pegatha stopped eating her fish for a moment to look round at Verity and hiss.

'It's just you she's not keen on,' I added.

Adam grinned and Verity looked furious.

'Come on, Adam,' she said, and they went off to join some of the older witchlings.

'Let's try the magic buffet table,' I said to Opal.

'What do I have to do?' she said. They clearly didn't have one at Cornish Cauldron coven.

'Just tell it what you'd like to eat. It can be anything at all, as weird as you want. We've got one at Coven Road and I don't think anyone's ever been able to ask for anything it couldn't manage – and believe me, I've tried!'

'I bet it doesn't know how to make sesame seed toast,' Opal said. 'That's my favourite.'

'Give it a go,' I said.

'I don't have to say a spell?'

'No, just tell it what you'd like.'

'Sesame toast, please,' Opal told the buffet

table, and immediately four pieces of sesame toast appeared on her plate.

'Too easy!' I said.

'You try, then.'

I didn't think anyone could trick the magic buffet table but I gave it a try anyway.

'Marmite . . . fingers . . . with cheese and mustard fudge.'

The buffet table produced a jar of Marmite and then some sponge-finger biscuits, followed by a

block of

cheese, a

tube of

mustard

and a

packet

of

fudge.

But just as I was thinking maybe I had tricked it after all, everything started mixing and whizzed together to make the dish I'd asked for.

Jezelda and Morgana passed us with matching bowls of berries from the berry fountain.

'Morning.'

'Morning.'

Not only did the twins look exactly the same but they liked to eat exactly the same food as well!

Opal tried very hard to think of something else the buffet table wouldn't be able to make easily. Finally she said, 'Rambutan jelly with banana pancakes, please.'

Even though neither of us had ever eaten rambutan jelly or banana pancakes, the buffet table knew what they were and produced two plates stacked high with both. I tried one of Opal's banana pancakes. It was delicious.

Pegatha saw Witch Hazel and ran over to her table. Opal and I hurried after her and found Pegatha looking up at Witch Hazel and saying, '*Miaow*, fish, *miaow*.' Then she stretched her

paws up to Witch Hazel, which is what she does when she wants to be picked up.

'I'm sorry about Pegatha bothering you,' I said.

'That's OK, she's no bother at all,' Witch Hazel said, smiling her jolly, crinkly smile. She picked Pegatha up and we all sat down at the top table.

Verity looked over at us and scowled, but it wasn't my fault that we were sitting with Witch Hazel – it was all Pegatha's doing!

Witch Hazel banged on a gong and instantly the dining cabin went silent.

'Our first spell-casting of the camp will take place in half an hour down by the turquoise lake,' she said.

Opal and I grinned at each other. I couldn't wait for our first spell-casting lesson to begin.

Chapter 8

When everyone had enjoyed their lunch, we all headed down the path to the turquoise lake where Witch Hazel was waiting for us beside her enormous cauldron.

'Some witches like to think of themselves as

white witches, others as green witches and some, of course, as black. But all magic is the same, it's just the intent of the user behind the spells that changes,' she told us. 'A white witch is someone who's vowed she will only use her magic for good.'

We all wanted to be white witches.

'I wouldn't want to hurt someone with one of my spells, even accidentally,' Jezelda said.

'I gave someone a warty nose once, but I didn't mean to,' I told her.

'I think it'd be OK to put a hex on someone bad, if they deserved it,' Verity said.

But no one else agreed with her. Hexes are spells that make something bad happen. My warty nose spell was a hex although I hadn't meant to cast that spell. It was before I even started learning magic. It was an accidental hex.

'Or maybe not,' she sighed.

'Today we're going to be learning the guiding light spell,' Witch Hazel said.

She selected wormwood, daisy petals, cinnamon and ginger from the ingredients laid out on the ground before her. Then she dropped

the ingredients into the cauldron and chanted, '*Beeardoa bdingal boardelerr begat.*'

Witch Hazel opened her hand as we all leant forward to look, and there, resting on her palm, was a ball of pure bright white light.

'Would anyone like to give it a try?' she asked us.

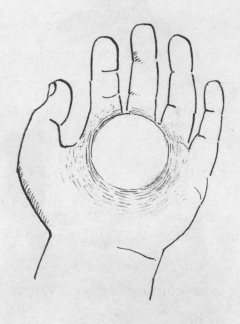

We all wanted to, of course, and soon everyone had created a ball of bright guiding light.

'Now you have created your guiding light, it will return to you whenever you say the spell. Even in the darkest of dark this light will shine bright,' Witch Hazel said, and she smiled her apple-cheeked, crinkly smile at us all.

When we got back to our tree house, Opal and I were so excited we were finishing off each other's sentences and talking over each other.

We were both agreed – Witch Camp was great!

In the afternoon we went swimming in the turquoise lake with the pink dolphins, while Witch Hazel sat in a deckchair with Pegatha on her lap.

'Aren't you coming in too, Witch Hazel?' Verity asked her.

'Oh no, I prefer to keep my feet firmly on dry land,' she said, and Pegatha miaowed her agreement.

'Angela would love the dolphins' pink colour,' I said to Opal.

'Who's Angela?' Opal asked me.

'A friend from school, whose favourite colour is pink.'

'Mine's black,' said Opal.

'Mine too,' I said.

After dinner we all gathered round the rainbow campfire and watched as little sparks of coloured stars flew out from the flames.

'Help yourselves to marshmallows when you're ready,' Witch Hazel said.

I'd never roasted a marshmallow before but Opal had. We each took a long stick and put a

marshmallow on the end of it and held the
stick into the flames at the edge of the fire.

'Don't let it catch fire if you can help it,' Opal said. 'And keep turning it so it gets toasty all over.'

Once our marshmallows were a soft golden brown, Opal said they were ready. 'But don't bite into them yet because they're too hot.'

We let them cool down a little and then bit into them. They were a little crunchy on the outside but warm and gooey inside.

'Mmmm mmmmm mmm,' we said at the same time.

The toasted marshmallows were so light and delicious. We ended up having ten each!

Pegatha wasn't allowed marshmallows but she'd eaten so much fish at dinner she probably wouldn't have had space for one anyway.

'Let's play Campfire Whispers,' Verity said.

'What a good idea, Verity,' said Witch Hazel and Verity beamed.

Witch Hazel whispered something in the ear of the witchling sitting on the ground next to her, and then that witchling whispered it to the witchling beside him. The whisper was passed on

and on round the circle until it
reached the very last witchling,
who was Morgana.
'What was the whisper?'
we all asked her.
Morgana frowned and said,
'Wise camel sees walnut?'
Witch Hazel giggled and shook her
head. She was laughing too much to
even speak. I liked how her eyes got all
screwed up when she laughed.
'Not "walnuts" – wasn't it "straw
hats"?' said Adam.
'I thought it was "blue moon",'
Razi said.
'No, it was "soon",' said Opal.
'What was it?' I asked Witch Hazel.
'Marshmallows under the moon,'
she said, laughing.

It wasn't anything like what we'd
ended up with!

Then it was Morgana's turn to start the
whispers and once again it was completely
different by the time it reached the last
witching.

'Gorgonzola tripe?' said Verity.

'Nope – "It's a beautiful night",'
Morgana told her.

Opal and I laughed and laughed.
It was after midnight when we got back
to our tree house cabin. We'd been so
busy I'd hardly thought about Lilith
and home all day. But as soon as I
got back I wanted to know what
she'd been up to and if she'd
missed me.

I took out the small crystal ball
and chanted the spell and, just like the

night before, Lilith's face appeared in there.

I told her all about the guiding light spell and the dolphins in the lake and toasting marshmallows.

'Pegatha is having a lovely time too,' I told Lilith. 'She spends most of her time being stroked by Witch Hazel!'

'You make me wish I was there too,' Lilith said.

'If you were, then Witch Camp would be so perfect I'd never want to leave,' I said.  'How are Mystica, Amelka, Brimalkin and Bazeeta?'

'They're fine,' Lilith said, and she went over to the bookcase so I could see them in my crystal ball, all sitting there as usual.

'I don't think they've even noticed that Pegatha and I have gone,' I said.

But Lilith shook her head. 'The house is quite, quite different without you two here,' she said, 'but I'm very glad you're having a good time.'

Chapter 9

My favourite part of the camp was learning new spells, but Opal was longing for the Gothic belly dancing.

'At last it's Gothic belly dancing,' she said, at the end of our first week. 'I can't wait!'

'Me neither,' I said, although no one could have been as excited about it as Opal was.

Our belly-dancing tutor, Princess Tamara, was very glamorous. She wore lots of black

eyeliner and had false eyelashes that were so long they made her eyes look really huge. She had feathers in her hair, dangly earrings and a ruby in her belly button. As well as bracelets on her wrists, Princess Tamara had bracelets on her ankles. Her toenails were painted black with little flecks of gold in them. Her skirt was long and floaty and her bodice had little gold tassels with bats at the end hanging from them.

Princess Tamara must have liked bats a lot because she also had some real-life tame bats that flew around her.

I'd never met a princess before and nor had Opal.

'Are you a real princess?' Opal asked her.

'We are all princes and princesses,' Princess Tamara said. 'And now it's time to dress like them.' Her many bracelets jingled as she

pointed to a jewelled pirates' chest. 'Help yourselves to costumes.'

We didn't need to be asked twice. Inside the chest there were lots of beautiful belly-dancing costumes, as well as bangles and tiaras and feathers, for us to choose from. Adam's costume

made him look like a character out of *Aladdin*. Verity pushed Jezelda out of the way so she could stand next to him instead.

'Don't forget to take a black scarf each,' Princess Tamara said.

She called them scarves but they weren't like woolly winter scarves — they were more like floaty summer sarongs.

Once we were all ready, the lesson began. As Princess Tamara played her small finger cymbals, which we were told were called zills, she danced and gave us instructions, and we copied what she did.

'Belly dancing has been going for as long as witchcraft,' Princess Tamara told us, as we swirled and twirled. 'Step and turn, left swing, right swing, scarves overhead . . .' Her bats flew around her. 'And now shimmy.'

We all wiggled our hips very fast, but only

Opal managed to move in time with the music.

'And walk like gods and goddesses!' Princess Tamara commanded us all.

I didn't know how gods and goddesses walked.

'How?' I shouted.

'Hold your head up and be proud of who you are,' Princess Tamara said. 'And remember, you're beautiful witchlings not timid little mice!'

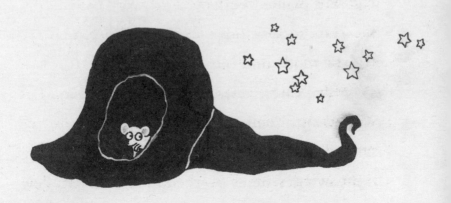

That made me laugh and it was hard to concentrate because I kept giggling. I think Pegatha might have liked me to be a mouse – but I didn't want to be a tasty snack for her!

Every single day of Witch Camp was filled with so much fun and magic that it seemed in no time at all that almost two weeks had gone by. I was very pleased with the white sage smudge stick I'd made and our cabin walls were now covered with spell-marbellised paper.

It was soon the eve of the Barley Moon and Lilith was setting off for the Sorcery Convention.

'You're sure you'll be all right while I'm away?' she said. 'I'll miss not hearing from you.'

Usually I chatted to Lilith in the crystal ball every day, but I was only supposed to contact Lilith at the Sorcery Convention if there was an emergency.

'Don't worry about me and Pegatha. Witch Camp is fantastic and nothing will go wrong,' I said.

Opal was sitting on her bed and she overheard me. She grinned and put her two thumbs up. I was very glad she was at the camp too. We'd been spell partners whenever we could, as well as practising our broomstick riding together. Pegatha liked her very much – almost as much as she liked Witch Hazel.

Chapter 10

'Banana pancakes, please,' I told the magic buffet table the next morning.

'Banana pancakes for me too, please,' said Opal.

Banana pancakes had been such a good idea

on the first day that Opal and I ate them for breakfast every day. Pegatha always had fish – all sorts of different fish – from catfish to dogfish. Some of them looked very strange.

We'd just sat down at our table when Witch Hazel came into the dining cabin.

'Good morning, my dears,' she said. 'I hope you all slept well?'

Usually as soon as Pegatha saw Witch Hazel she ran over to her. Most breakfast times were spent with Pegatha sitting on Witch Hazel's lap and purring – but not today. Today Pegatha just carried on eating her fish.

I'd put on my orange pendant with the black flecks inside it and Witch Hazel immediately noticed.

'What a pretty
necklace,' she said,
coming over.

'Thanks, my mum
gave it to me,' I told her. 'It's made from —'

'Amber,' Witch Hazel said. 'It's very
powerful.' As she spoke she bent down to stroke
Pegatha and then the strangest thing happened:
Pegatha actually hissed at her!

I couldn't understand it. Witch Hazel was
usually one of Pegatha's absolute favourite
people.

'I'm so sorry,' I said. 'I don't know what's got
into her this morning.'

I picked Pegatha up and wouldn't let her go
even when she tried to
wriggle away.

Witch Hazel stretched
her hand out to Pegatha

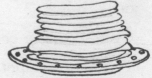

again but Pegatha flexed her claws and arched her back.

'Maybe she's got a tummy-ache,' I said. It was the first thing I could think of. 'She has been eating an awful lot of fish since we got here.'

'Perhaps,' said Witch Hazel, but she looked doubtful.

'I'll see if she wants to have a lie down in our cabin,' I said, and I hurried over to the door with her.

'Fish!' Pegatha yeowled. 'Fish! Fish!'

The magic buffet table obediently produced

three plates of different fishes for Pegatha but that wasn't what she meant at all.

'Why were you so nasty to Witch Hazel?' I asked her, as we went through the tree house cabin door.

'Fish,' Pegatha said, her ears flattened.

'It was very rude of you,' I said.

Pegatha hopped onto the dresser and turned her back on me.

'I think all the attention you've been getting has gone to your head,' I told her furry back.

'Fish,' Pegatha said, so softly I almost didn't hear her.

'Maybe you'd better stay here and have a rest while I go to my snake-charming lesson.'

Pegatha jumped off the dresser and onto my pillow where she curled herself up in a ball.

'Is Pegatha all right?' Opal asked, coming in behind us. She sounded worried.

'I think so,' I said. But I wasn't really sure.

I'd have liked to tell Lilith what had happened in case she knew what was wrong, but it was almost time for our lesson to begin and I didn't want to disturb her at the Sorcery Convention.

'She'll probably be back to her usual self after she's had a sleep,' Opal said, and I nodded, although I didn't think Pegatha was really all that sleepy.

Opal and I hurried down to the turquoise lake where the rest of the witchlings were waiting.

Our snake-charming instructor, Salandera, gave us each a snake-charming flute. But however much I blew into mine, my snake refused to poke its head out of its basket.

Soon all the other witchlings' snakes were

swaying from side to side, but there was still no sign of my one. I'm not very musical and my flute playing wasn't very tuneful – but still!

Salandera peered into my basket. My snake was curled in a coil at the bottom of the basket, fast asleep!

'Wake up!' Salandera commanded it and my snake wound its way to the top of the basket.

'Play,' Salandera told me.

I played as loudly as I could and my snake jumped out of the basket and tried to slither away from the noise I was making!

'Catch it, quickly!' Salandera shouted, and I ran after my snake.

It slithered past Witch Hazel's closed cauldron and I just managed to grab its tail before it went down a rabbit hole.

'Got you!'

It tried to wriggle away but I held on and took it back to Salandera.

I put my snake back in its basket but Salandera said I shouldn't play my flute to it any more. 'You just watch everyone else – no more snake-charming for you. It's far too exciting!'

Opal and I laughed and laughed about the

snake afterwards as we hurried back to our tree house.

Pegatha was waiting for us at the bottom of the tree and I crouched down to stroke her soft fur.

'Fish,' she said, as she nuzzled her face into my neck. All was forgiven.

In the afternoon we had a spell-casting lesson with Witch Hazel. Previously Pegatha had come along to all my spell-casting lessons but today she only followed Opal and me halfway to the turquoise lake and then she turned and ran back the way she'd come.

'Pegatha!' I called after her, but she didn't come back.

It didn't matter, of course. Pegatha could go wherever she wanted but usually she was like a little shadow to me. Maybe she really was feeling off-colour.

'Today we're going to learn how to cast hexes,' Witch Hazel said.

'Oh goody,' said Verity. 'Only, I thought we weren't allowed to do bad spells like hexes and curses? You told us —'

Witch Hazel didn't let her finish. 'I think it's important for witchlings to learn about all sorts of magic – so they can make the choice of how to use magic for themselves,' she said. 'The best hexes play on our fears. So, what are you frightened of, witchlings? What makes you shiver and shake? What wouldn't you, or would you, wish on your worst enemy?'

Ophelia put her hand up. 'Princess Tamara's bats scared me,' she said. 'But giant vampire bats would be even worse.'

'Good. Anyone else?' Witch Hazel asked us.

'I'm frightened of being trapped all alone in the dark,' Verity said.

'I'm scared of crocodiles that come up from the sewers,' said Adam.

'Ghosts and zombies,' said Opal.

Jezelda said she shook at the sight of a rat and Mia told us that she always checked under her bed in case there was something unnamed but horrible lurking in the darkness. Brett and Razi were both scared of thunderstorms and Kye hated snakes.

'Snake-charming this morning was torture,' he said.

'I'd do
anything to avoid
touching a toad,'
Toby said, and we
all looked round
in surprise.

'But toads are supposed to be witches' familiars!' Verity said. 'They often accompany witches wherever they go!'

'Not me!' he told her.

'I have nightmares about sinking into thick squishy quicksand that won't let me go,' said Morgana.

I was soon the only one who hadn't said what I was most scared of. I didn't want to tell Witch Hazel my secret fear, which was that something bad would happen to Lilith and I wouldn't be able to live with her any more.

'What are you most frightened of, Bella

Donna?' Witch Hazel now asked, and she stared at me so hard it felt like her eyes were trying to probe my brain.

'Spiders,' I lied. It was much better to pretend I was scared of something that didn't make my stomach ache when I thought about it.

'That's what you are most afraid of?' said Witch Hazel. She didn't sound like she believed me.

'Yes, I am. Anything creepy crawly terrifies me, especially spiders,' I said, although this wasn't totally true. I don't like creepy crawlies much and I wouldn't want to pick a spider up, but my friend Sam introduced me to all sorts of bugs when we were living at the children's home

together, and although
I wouldn't want a spider
as a pet, I wasn't all that
scared of them.

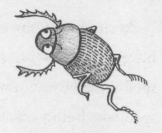

It was hard to be
scared when Sam
was so full of admiration
for any sort of bug!

'There are many ways to cast hexes,' Witch Hazel told us, 'but the way I prefer to do it is to pass on my very worst fears to the person I'm hexing. You all know how important the intention behind a spell is and your fear gives the hex even greater power.'

Opal put her hand up. 'Excuse me, Witch Hazel, but what ingredients do we need for hex spells?'

'Only one,' Witch Hazel told us. 'An item that belongs to the spell's recipient.'

As she spoke, she stared at me because I must have looked a bit confused. I'd never done a spell where something from the person who the spell was being cast on was needed before.

'Aren't we going to use the cauldron today, then?' I asked her. I noticed it still had its lid on.

'No, not today. I'm resting it from all the spellwork it's had to do,' Witch Hazel said. 'What we do need, though, is something to cast the hex spell on.'

She pointed to a nearby purple butterfly bush.

'That will do,' she said,

and she plucked a leaf from it. 'Repeat the spell after me.'

Witch Hazel kept pointing at the bush as she chanted, '*Diasasras delondola diamara!*'

Everyone obediently chanted the hex spell words after her and pointed at the bush too. It felt odd learning how to cast a spell that was aimed at deliberately doing harm. But I cast the hex like everyone else. '*Diasasras delondola diamara!*'

Only the hex spell worked far too well.

The bush, that moments before had been full of purple flowers, was quickly turning brown and dying, but even worse, the butterflies that had been in the bush lay dead on the ground.

'Noooo!' I cried, when I saw what we had done. I felt sick. 'How could you make us do that?' I asked Witch Hazel.

At Coven Road we never hurt anything. Lilith would never have taught us a spell like this.

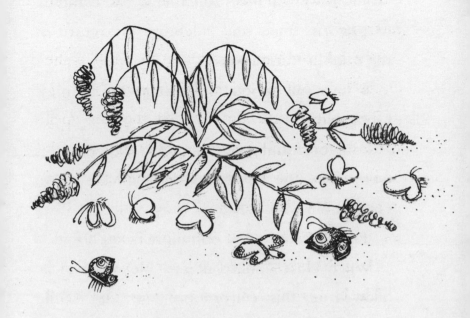

But Witch Hazel simply dropped
the leaf from the bush on the
ground and acted like she
hadn't even heard me.

'Any spell cast by thirteen
witches, or witchlings, has
great power,' she said.

'Tonight we will meet together at the campfire to perform spells and celebrate the return of the mighty Barley Moon.'

'I love full moon welcoming ceremonies,' Opal said.

I did too, usually, but I couldn't drag my eyes away from the butterflies lying on the grass. How could we have done that?

'I don't want to cast any more hexes,' I said.

Witch Hazel looked at me. 'No cats will be allowed at this celebration,' she said. 'Bella Donna, you must stay behind and look after Pegatha.'

I should have been upset to be missing the ceremony but the truth was I wasn't. I couldn't help suddenly feeling very uneasy about Witch Hazel and the wicked spell she'd made us cast.

Chapter 11

After supper it was time for the full moon celebration to begin.

'Not Witch Hazel's favourites any more then, Bella and Pegatha,' Verity said, laughing as the rest of them got ready in the cabin.

I was busy looking for my witch mobile. Usually it hung by my bed but it wasn't there now. I looked behind my chest of drawers and under the bed but I couldn't see it.

'Has anyone seen my witch mobile?' I asked. 'It was right here.'

But no one had.

'I'll help you look,' Opal said, but she couldn't see it either.

'I think Witch Hazel's right, you know. I'm glad Pegatha won't be dropping her fleas and cat fur all over the Barley Moon celebration,' Verity said. She was all dressed up and ready to go.

'You're just as likely to have fleas as Pegatha is,' I told Verity crossly, and Pegatha hissed at her.

'I'll stay behind with you, Bella,' Opal said. But I didn't want her to miss out.

'No, you go.' I told her.

'If you're sure?'

I knew how much she really wanted to go to the celebration.

'I'm sure.'

Opal left with the others and I stroked Pegatha and wished I knew where my witch mobile had gone. Then I thought about how unfair it was that we had to miss out. I didn't really like Witch Hazel very much any more.

I wanted to tell Lilith about what had happened, but I was only supposed to get in touch with her at the Sorcery Convention in an emergency, and this didn't really seem like one.

I'd never been to a Barley Moon celebration and I really wanted to see what it was like and also what spells were performed. But just because I wasn't invited didn't mean I couldn't go. I decided to secretly follow them.

I put Pegatha down on my bed and she curled up on my pillow.

'I'll be back soon,' I told her, and I left the cabin and climbed down the tree house ladder.

Outside the Barley Moon shone brightly and I could see the rainbow campfire just ahead of me. Only, it wasn't rainbow-coloured any more. The flames were black and red and the fire looked angry.

I hid behind a tree so I could see what was

happening without being seen. But as I got closer, the celebration didn't really seem to be much of a celebration. None of the witchlings looked like they were having any fun. In fact, their faces all looked oddly blank as the shadows of the red and black flames flickered over them. Witch Hazel stood in the centre, close to the fire, with the witchlings in a circle around her. She looked up at the moon as she raised her hands above her head.

'We, the new thirteen of thirteen, welcome in the Barley Moon,' she said, and all the witchlings raised their hands and repeated what she said.

Then I couldn't believe my ears. Witch Hazel started to chant the hex spell. '*Diasasras delondola diamara!*'

'No!' I gasped. I didn't want anything else to be hurt like the butterflies had been.

Witch Hazel heard my gasp, turned and pointed straight at me. 'Hex her!' she shouted.

I didn't think they would, but all of the witchlings raised their fingers at exactly the same time. Their faces were blank, as if they were in a trance, or under a spell, as they pointed their fingers at me and began to chant. *'Diasasras delondola diamara!'*

I turned and ran. But no sooner had I started running than the hexes started working. I screamed as the sky rumbled with thunder and there was a crack of lightning. The camp turned from lush green fields with colourful wild flowers into a muddy, fog-shrouded swamp. My feet sank into the squishy, stinky quicksand that had been Morgana's greatest fear. The sky grew eerily dark.

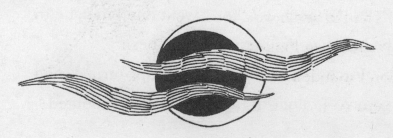

'*Beeardoa bdingal boardelerr begat!*' I
shouted, and my ball of guiding light appeared in
my hand.

But although I could now see where I was
running, in many ways it made everything
worse. Now I could also see
Ophelia's vampire bats flying
around my head, and even

Sam
would
have been wary of
Kye's hex snakes and
Jezelda's rats.

'They're not really
real,' I told myself.
'They're just hexes.'
But they looked
and sounded
very real.

I narrowly missed running straight into a large toad that blocked my path. A crocodile opened its jaws beside me. In the distance ghosts swirled and zombies staggered towards me.

I remembered what Sam had said about not showing fear. I tried to think what the opposite of looking scared might be and suddenly I knew. I threw back my head and laughed as loudly as I could.

At first my laughter sounded forced and fake, but the crocodile disappeared! I laughed properly at that, and then the snakes and spiders and rats and bats and ghosts and zombies all faded away too. Even the swamp mud dried out and the thunderclouds rolled away. It looked like my laughter was working!

Once the hex creatures had gone, I heard a woeful mewling instead — a mewling that I would have recognised anywhere.

'Pegatha,' I cried. She was running towards me and I scooped her up in my arms. 'Oh, Pegatha.'

I could feel her heart beating very fast. Her little rough tongue licked my face.

'I'm so pleased to see you,' I said, as I hugged her to me.

I didn't know what was happening or why Witch Hazel had made the witchlings cast their hex spells. All I knew was that something was terribly wrong and I was very, very frightened.

'If only I had my crystal ball, then I could ask Lilith to help us,' I said.

But the crystal ball was still in the tree house cabin and I didn't dare go back to find it. It would be the first place Witch Hazel would look for me.

In the distance I saw a blur heading towards us – fast. As it got closer, I recognised that it was my broomstick and I sighed with relief. I'd know my broomstick anywhere. It must have heard me scream and have flown out of the broomstick rack to find us.

Pegatha and I climbed on as soon as my broomstick reached us.

'Thank you,' I said, stroking its branch.

But on the horizon I could see more broomsticks heading towards us.

'Fish,' Pegatha told the broomstick. 'Fish, fish, fiiiiiiish . . .'

I couldn't understand what she meant but my broomstick did.

It flew as fast as it could in the opposite direction, across the field, over the lake and to the edge of the Ice Cave where it came to a wobbly stop.

Pegatha hopped off the broomstick and raced to the door. Luckily I remember almost every spell that I hear, and knew the spell that Witch Hazel had used to open it. '*Corasalis chanali cartosos,*' I chanted, and the huge ice door creaked open.

'Fiiiissh!' Pegatha said urgently as she raced ahead of me, and I ran after her, holding my broomstick. Pegatha ran down the narrow tunnel, stopped at the ice lake, licked her cold paws and then looked up at me.

'What? What is it?' I said.

'Fish?' said Pegatha, and then batted at the snowflake her word turned into. When I still didn't understand, she stepped out onto the ice lake and sat down.

'Oh,' I said, and a single snowflake flew up into the air.

Pegatha was such a clever cat!

Lilith had said if a crystal ball wasn't available then a piece of glass, or even ice, would do. I stared into the ice lake and chanted, '*Hoooonyaza ... hekingabaal ... hallazareti ...*

'Please let it work, oh please, please let it work,' I wished, as I bit at my bottom lip.

As I stared into the ice lake, I saw swirls of blue and white, and then suddenly I was looking at a beautiful room with a big fireplace. There, in the middle of it, I saw Lilith brushing her hair.

'Lilith,' I called out. 'Lilith!'

Lilith looked around in surprise, and then looked right at me with wide eyes.

'Bella! What on earth are you doing in my mirror?' she said. 'Are you all right? Has something happened? Is Pegatha OK?'

'Pegatha's here with me – she's fine,' I told her, 'but Witch Hazel's turned bad and she and the other witchlings put hexes on us. We're hidden in the Ice Cave. She said she was making a new thirteen of thirteen with the other witchlings.'

I heard footsteps in the ice corridor behind me. I hadn't known how to close the ice door behind us and now someone was coming! Pegatha hissed.

'I think she's found us. Please come. Come quickly!' I cried, but I was so afraid that I lost my concentration, and the ice went as blank as a mirror once more.

'I should have known it would be you causing me all this trouble,' Witch Hazel said as she crossed the cave and stood right in front of me.

She had my missing witch mobile in her hand. The other witchlings stood behind her, but they looked confused, like they were sleepwalking.

As she spoke, I looked down at the ice and that's when I saw her true face reflected there. It was thin with hollow cheeks where Witch Hazel's face had been round with cheeks like rosy apples. She had angry frown lines instead of Witch Hazel's crinkly laughter ones. But it was still a face I knew.

'Rosina Rowan,' I gasped.

We'd met before when she had tried to take over Coven Road and I'd stopped her by trapping her in amber.

Pegatha hissed again as Rosina laughed her evil cackle. 'You had no idea it was me, you silly witchling! Only your cat knew something was different!'

Rosina must have cast an imitation spell to make herself look like Witch Hazel, but the ice showed the truth.

'She's not Witch Hazel,' I shouted.

'Of course she's Witch Hazel,' said Jezelda sleepily. 'Look at her!'

'No, she isn't. She's a bad witch called Rosina Rowan,' I said.

'What are you talking about, Bella Donna?' said Verity. 'Rosina Rowan's not here. Zorelda sent her away, remember?'

'No – look!' I said, and I pointed at the ice lake where Rosina's true face was reflected.

'Don't look!' Rosina commanded them.

But it was too late. The witchlings crowded round trying to get a better peek. As more and more of them realised the truth, the illusion got weaker and weaker until Rosina didn't look or sound anything like Witch Hazel any more.

'Nooooooo!' shrieked Rosina, and she pointed at me. 'You! You've ruined everything – again!'

And with a puff of black smoke she was gone, and all that was left behind was my witch mobile and her cloak lying crumpled on the ground. I picked up my mobile and put it in my pocket.

'Bella!' a voice called out, and I looked round to see Lilith running down the ice corridor, closely followed by Zorelda.

I ran to Lilith and she hugged me tightly

while Pegatha miaowed and said 'Fish' every now and again.

'Are you all right?' Lilith asked me.

I nodded and told her about Rosina Rowan's illusion spell.

'I blame myself,' Zorelda said. 'I should have known we wouldn't have seen the last of her. No coven would have her, so she must have decided to create a new one from the Witch Camp's witchlings.'

'Where is she now?' Lilith asked me.

'She disappeared,' I said. 'All that's left is her cloak.'

Zorelda picked the cloak up. 'This will be enough for the Witches' Council to summon and punish her,' she said.

'What's going on? Where are we? What are you doing here, Auntie Lilith?' Verity said.

'I feel really weird,' said Jezelda.

'Like I've just woken up,' agreed Morgana, as she rubbed at her eyes.

'What happened to us?' said Adam, scratching his head.

All of the witchlings looked dazed and like they'd just come out of a deep sleep.

'You had a spell put on you,' I told them. 'By a very powerful witch.'

My hand went up to my amber pendant. I had managed to defeat Rosina Rowan before. Perhaps that's why she had wanted me stay away for the evening. Although I had truly thought she was Witch Hazel at first, Pegatha was the only one who hadn't been deceived.

'She must have realised you were too powerful for her to control, Bella Donna,' Morgana said. Jezelda nodded beside her.

I told Zorelda it was really all thanks to Pegatha. Without her and my broomstick I didn't like to think what would have happened.

'But where's the real Witch Hazel?' Opal said. 'What's happened to her?'

I hoped Rosina hadn't put one of her hex spells on her. Then I remembered the lid on the giant cauldron. Witch Hazel's cauldron never used to have the lid on it at the beginning of camp.

'I think I know where Witch Hazel is,' I said, and we all flew back to the turquoise lake.

Once we'd got there, I jumped off my broomstick and ran over to the cauldron. I tried to lift the lid but it wouldn't budge and I didn't know what spell to use. But Zorelda did.

'*Hereshaza halimacar tiffusara,*' she chanted, and the cauldron lid floated up into the air.

We looked inside and there was Witch Hazel, curled up and fast asleep. Pegatha purred with happiness as Lilith and I helped Witch Hazel out of the cauldron.

'What happened?' she said sleepily. 'How did I end up inside my own cauldron?'

Zorelda dropped red agate, rosemary and rue along with a protective aniseed flower into the rainbow campfire's flames to help restore Witch Hazel's memory.

Pegatha miaowed and stretched to show she wanted to be picked up as soon as Witch Hazel was back to her old self.

'Merry meet, Pegatha,' Witch Hazel said, cuddling Pegatha to her. 'If it wasn't for you, Bella Donna, we would have all been in serious trouble.' Then she smiled at Lilith. 'She's such a brave girl and knows what's right and wrong. You must be so proud of your daughter.'

'Thank you, yes I am,' Lilith said, and she squeezed my hand.

A huge grin crept across my face.

Of course there was only one thing to do now that Rosina Rowan had been defeated and the real Witch Hazel had been found. Fortunately it's something that doesn't take any time at all to get ready if you're a witch.

'Celebration party?' Witch Hazel said, and we all thought that was a very good idea indeed.

In no time at all, the rainbow campfire was shooting out multi-coloured stars and the buffet table was working overtime. Soon everyone was chatting and laughing and dancing.

'I always knew the other Witch Hazel wasn't really Witch Hazel,' Verity said. 'The real Witch Hazel would never have let us do hexes.' She sounded a little bit disappointed.

'Want to dance, Verity?' Adam said, coming

over to us, and Verity suddenly grinned like a Cheshire cat, which is a very big grin indeed, as she went to dance with him.

I introduced Opal to Lilith, and Lilith said she was very glad I'd made a new friend and maybe

Opal would like to come and visit us sometime.

'I'd love it!' Opal said. Then she looked round. 'Where's Pegatha?' she asked me, and I smiled and pointed. Pegatha was curled up in Witch Hazel's lap, fast asleep.

The next morning I packed my suitcase. It was time to go home.

Witch Hazel stroked Pegatha and hugged me. 'Goodbye, Bella Donna. It was a pleasure getting to know you and Pegatha,' she said. 'And thank you for, you know . . . the rescuing. You should be proud of your strength of character. You're a very fine witchling.'

I hugged her back. If I had a granny, I'd want her to be exactly like Witch Hazel with her crinkly smile.

Pegatha hopped onto my broomstick and Lilith and Verity climbed onto theirs.

'Up, up and away!' I shouted, and behind me I heard Pegatha agree, although what she actually said was, 'Fish!'

As we flew up into the air, my broomstick blossomed with hundreds of wild flowers and I knew it was pleased to be going home too.

'See you at Witch Camp next year, Bella,' Opal shouted after us.

'After all that's happened, you still want to come again?' I called back.

'You bet!' She laughed. 'Witch Camp is just about the most exciting, amazing, magical place in the whole world!'

And she was right about that.

Have you read all of Bella Donna's adventures?

Bella Donna

Coven Road

Most girls dream of being a princess, but
Bella Donna has always longed to be a
witch. The only thing she wants more is
to find a family to take her out of the
children's home where she lives.
But no one seems quite right,
until she meets Lilith.

With Lilith's help, will Bella Donna
be able to make both of her
secret wishes come true?

Bella Donna

Too Many Spells

Bella Donna appears to be a regular girl at a
regular school with her regular friends,
but she has a secret — she is really
a young witch!

She's working hard at learning
her spells, and is desperate to
win the Spell-Casting Contest.
But when strange things start
happening at school, Bella begins
to wonder if she can really
control her magic . . .

Bella Donna

Witchling

Bella Donna is a witchling – a young witch who must keep her powers a secret, and only use magic when she's at home in the enchanted Coven Road.

But it's hard to stick to the rules when magic is such fun. There are so many things Bella can't quite resist, like flying on her broomstick and trying out some very special spells . . .

Bella Donna

Cat Magic

Where is Pegatha?
Bella Donna's favourite cat goes missing and
Bella tries every magic spell she can think of
to find her. All the other witches in Coven Road
get on their broomsticks to join the search,
but with no luck.

There's only one
explanation –
someone must have
put a spell on
Pegatha.
But who,
and why?

Coming soon

Bella Donna

Bella Bewitched

Everything is going topsy-turvy
for Bella Donna.
A new spell gives her the chance to
see the world differently –
and swapping bodies with Pegatha
is a very surprising adventure!

Bella Donna

Join Bella Donna online!

Explore and
download games,
puzzles,
activities,
and much more!

BellaDonnaOnline.co.uk